W9-AXC-905

LITTLE HOUSE
Laura Ingalls Wilder

MY FIRST LITTLE HOUSE BOOKS

PRAIRIE DAY

ADAPTED FROM THE LITTLE HOUSE BOOKS

By Laura Ingalls Wilder

Illustrated by Renée Graef

HARPERCOLLINS PUBLISHERS

For Maxfield
—R.G.

Illustrations prepared with the help of Cathy Holly.

Prairie Day Text adapted from Little House on the Prairie, copyright 1935, 1963 Little House Heritage Trust. Illustrations copyright © 1997 by Renée Graef. Manufactured in China. All rights reserved. Library of Congress Cataloging-in-Publication Data Wilder, Laura Ingalls, 1867–1957. Prairie day : adapted from the Little house books by Laura Ingalls Wilder / illustrated by Renée Graef. p. cm. — (My first Little house books) Summary: A little girl and her pioneer family travel westward to find a new home on the prairie. ISBN 0-06-443504-0 (pbk.). [1. 2. Frontier and pioneer life—Fiction. 2. Family life—Fiction.] I. Graef, Renée, ill. II. Title. III. Series. PZ7.W6461Pr 1997 96-14361 [E]—dc20 CIP AC HarperCollins®, ▰®, and Little House® are trademarks of HarperCollins Publishers Inc. Visit us on the World Wide Web! www.littlehousebooks.com

Illustrations for the My First Little House Books are inspired by the work of Garth Williams with his permission, which we gratefully acknowledge.

Once upon a time, a little girl named Laura, her Pa and her Ma, her big sister, Mary, her baby sister, Carrie, and their good old bulldog, Jack, headed west in their covered wagon for the prairie.

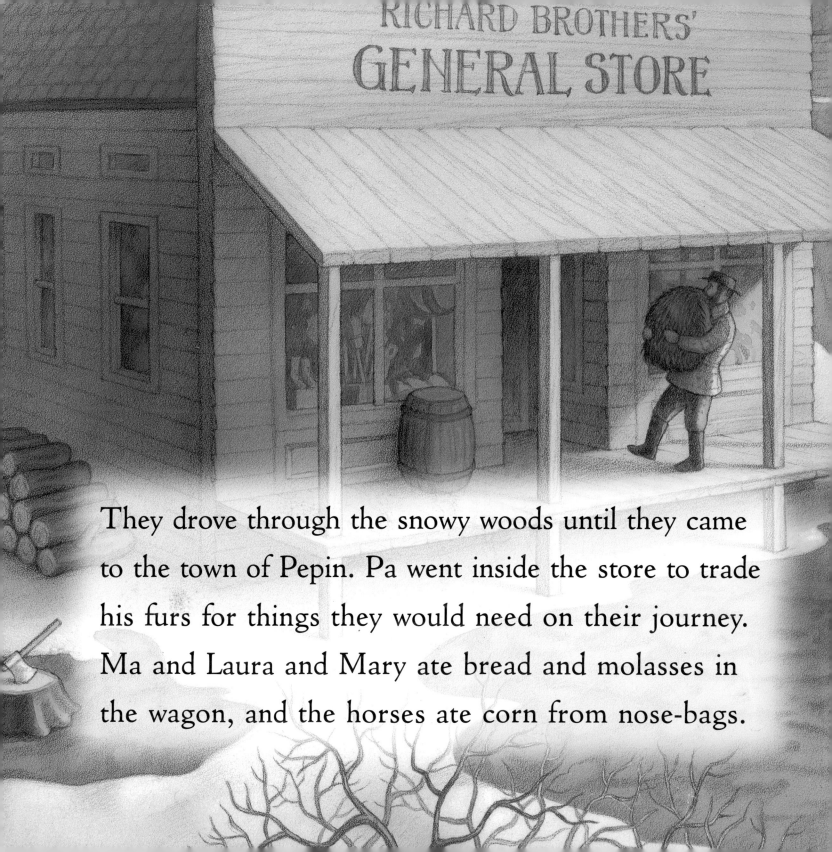

They drove through the snowy woods until they came
to the town of Pepin. Pa went inside the store to trade
his furs for things they would need on their journey.
Ma and Laura and Mary ate bread and molasses in
the wagon, and the horses ate corn from nose-bags.

Soon they reached a big lake that stretched flat and smooth and white all the way to the edge of the gray sky.

The horses' hoofs clop-clopped, and the wagon wheels crunched as Pa drove the wagon onto the ice. Laura didn't like it, but she knew nothing could hurt her while Pa and Jack were there.

At last the wagon came to a slope of earth, and there stood a little log house among the trees. It was a tiny house for travelers to camp in. That night Laura and Mary and Ma and Baby Carrie slept in front of the fire, while Pa slept outside to guard the wagon and the horses.

Every day after that they traveled as far as the horses could go, and every night they made camp in a new place. They crossed too many creeks to count and drove across long wooden bridges. They saw strange woods and even stranger country with no trees.

After many days and nights they came to the Kansas prairie, a flat land with rippling grass and a great big sky.

The wind blew Laura's straight brown hair and Mary's golden curls every-which-way.

Soon Laura and Mary were tired of traveling with nothing new to look at. Poor Jack was tired, too. At last Pa stopped the wagon and said, "We'll camp here a day or two." He unharnessed the horses, and they rolled back and forth and over until the feeling of the harness was all gone from their backs.

Pa cleared a space in the prairie grass for a fire,
and Laura and Mary helped Ma get supper. Pa
brought water from a creek, and Ma mixed the water
with cornmeal and salt and patted it into little cakes.
She fried slices of fat salt pork in the iron spider.
The cakes baked, the meat fried, and Laura grew
hungrier and hungrier.

At last supper was ready. Pa and Ma sat on the wagon-seat and Laura and Mary sat on the wagon tongue. Each of them had a tin plate and a steel knife and a steel fork. Ma had a tin cup and Pa had a tin cup, and Baby Carrie had a little one of her own, but Mary and Laura had to share their tin cup.

While they were eating supper, the prairie became
dark and still, and soon it was past bedtime. Mary
and Laura put their long nightgowns on, said their
prayers, and crawled into their little bed in the wagon.

The next morning, they all sat on the clean grass and ate pancakes and bacon and molasses. All around them tiny birds were swinging and singing in tiny voices. "Dickie, dickie," Laura called to them.

"Eat your breakfast, Laura," Ma said. "You must mind your manners, even if we are a hundred miles from anywhere."

After everything in the camp was tidy, Pa went hunting and Laura and Mary went exploring. It was fun to run through the tall grass, in the sunshine and the wind. There were huge rabbits and tiny dickie-birds everywhere, and little brown-striped gophers. Mary and Laura wanted to catch a gopher to take to Ma. Laura ran and ran and couldn't catch one. They took some flowers to Ma instead of a gopher.

Before long, the sun was low, and Pa was coming across the prairie. Laura jumped up and ran to him and hippety-hopped through the tall grass beside him.

That night after supper, Pa's fiddle sang in the starlight. The large bright stars hung down from the sky, and Laura thought the stars might be singing too. Soon it was time for little girls to be in bed, so Ma tied on their nightcaps and tucked them into bed. Tomorrow they must be on their way again to find their new little house on the prairie.